Y0-CAE-996

My Grandson Lew

by
**CHARLOTTE
ZOLOTOW**

**pictures by
WILLIAM
PÈNE DU BOIS**

An URSULA NORDSTROM Book

Harper & Row, Publishers

To Joseph M. Arnof

Lewis woke in the night.
His mother heard him call.
What is it? she said,
sitting on the edge of his bed.

5

I miss Grandpa, Lewis said.

You miss him! said Lew's mother.
You were two when he died.
Now you're six
and you never asked for him before.

I think about him though, said Lew.
I remember him.
He had a beard
and it scratched when he kissed me.

What else, asked his mother,
what else do you remember?

Blue eyes
said Lewis.
I remember how his beard scratched
but I remember his eyes more.
He gave me eye-hugs
nights like this
when I woke up
and called.

Grandpa came in the night?
asked Lew's mother.

Yes, said Lew.
I'd call
and instead of you
Grandpa would come.

He had a long white bathrobe
and he'd look like a sailboat
coming in the door.

He'd lean over
and pick me up.
His beard scratched
and then he'd smile
and hug me.

He'd carry me into the other room
and walk up and down
and hum a sort of tune.
I could hear it
rumbling
in his chest.

I never knew this
Lewis's mother said.
What else do you remember?

He wasn't here much
said Lewis.

He came
when you and Father
went away.

I remember him
mostly at night
but once
in the daytime
we went out.
He carried me
up a lot of stairs
and we looked at
pictures
with bright colors
and one of an ocean
and a sky.

The museum!
said Lew's mother.
You do remember.
He told me later
you fell asleep
on the way home.

You never talked about it.
I never knew you remembered him at all.

I only half remember
Lewis said.
But I can still feel
him carrying me.
His arms were strong
and he smelled of powder
and tobacco.

Once he let me warm my hands
around his pipe.

I waited
but he hasn't come back.
And I miss him.

You never asked about him though
Lew's mother said.

He always came back
Lew said
without me saying anything.
I've been waiting for him.

He lived a long way from here
Lew's mother explained.
You never asked
so I never told you
Grandpa died.

I want him to come back.
I miss him, Lewis said.
I have been waiting for him
and I miss him especially tonight.

I do too
said Lew's mother.
But you made him come back
for me tonight
by telling me what you remember.

I'll tell you
something I remember too.

What? Lew asked.

He always laughed
when he was happy,
Lew's mother said.
When you were born
he laughed out loud
when he looked at you.
My grandson, he said.
My grandson, Lew.

He took you out of the nurse's arms
and handled you
as though you were a kitten.

He touched your hair
and your cheek
and smiled at you
as though you and he
were alone in the room.
My grandson, he kept saying.
My grandson, Lew.

Then he leaned over
and put you on the bed
beside me.

He kissed me too.
Any time you want
he said
I'll come
to stay with him.
I know how to take care of babies
because I took care of you.

And whenever
your father and I
went away
Grandpa took the plane back here
to stay with you.

But I never knew
he never told me
you called him in the night.

He liked to paint.
That's why he took you to the museum.
He's too little, I said.
He won't remember.

But I do, said Lew.
I remember him taking me.

I miss him.

So do I, Lew's mother said.
But now
we will remember him together
and neither of us
will be so lonely
as we would be
if we had to remember him
alone.